THREE
MONKS

D1551170

Adaptation from the film by Shanghai Animation and Film Studio
Copyright © 2009 Shanghai Press and Publishing Development Company

All rights reserved. Unauthorized reproduction, in any manner, is prohibited.

This book is edited and designed by the Editorial Committee of *Cultural China* series

Managing Directors: Wang Youbu, Xu Naiqing
Editorial Director: Wu Ying
Editor: Yang Xiaohe

Adaptation by Sanmu Tang
Translation by Wu Ying

Cover Design: Wang Wei
Interior Design: J-Point Studio

ISBN: 978-1-60220-973-2

Address any comments about *Three Monks* to:

Better Link Press
99 Park Ave
New York, NY 10016
USA
or
Shanghai Press and Publishing Development Company
F 7 Donghu Road, Shanghai, China (200031)
Email: comments_betterlinkpress@hotmail.com

Printed in China by Shanghai Donnelley Printing Co. Ltd.

1 2 3 4 5 6 7 8 9 10

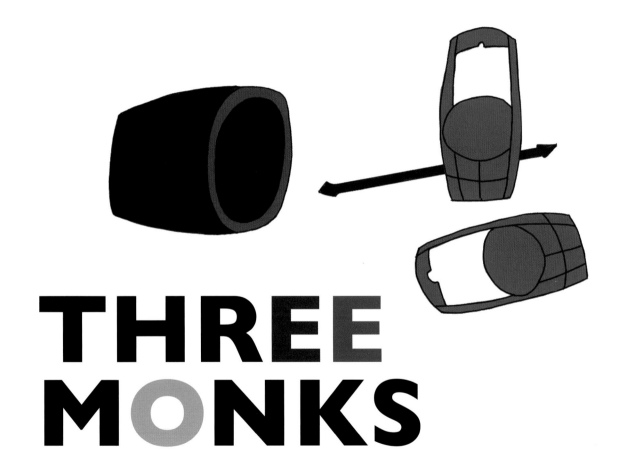

THREE MONKS

Better Link Press

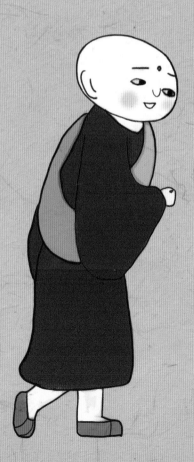

One day, a little monk went to live in a small temple on a hill.

During the daytime, he worshipped Buddha and fetched water. At night he chanted Buddhist scripture. He lived an untroubled and peaceful life.

A few days later, there came a tall and thin monk to the small temple.

The two monks greeted each other.

The little monk offered the tall monk the water he had fetched to drink.

When the water had all gone, the tall monk shouldered two buckets and went to fetch more water.

The little monk was happy about this, and the
tall monk settled down in the small temple.

Thinking that he was being short-changed by going to fetch water alone, the tall monk asked the little monk to come with him to help carry the water.

So, together, the two monks worshipped Buddha and fetched water during the daytime, and meditated and chanted Buddhist scripture at night. Although there was friction over petty matters from time to time, life continued peacefully.

Time went by. Then, one day,
a fat monk came to the temple.

The three monks greeted one another.

The little monk and the tall monk offered drinking water to the fat monk, who drank up all their water in one gulp.

After drinking up all the water, the fat
monk dropped off to sleep.

Both the little monk and the tall monk were angry with the fat monk and asked him to go and fetch some more water for them.

No sooner had the water been fetched than the three monks drank it all up.

Then, none of them would talk to each other. No one wanted to be the one to go and fetch water. Each beat his wooden block and chanted Buddhist sutra by himself.

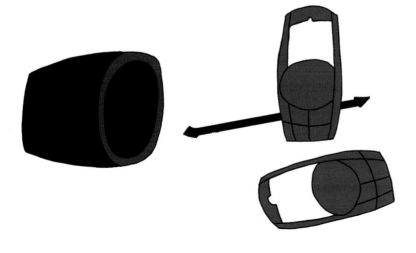

When night fell, the mice came out to play mischief and knocked over a candlestick. The temple caught fire.

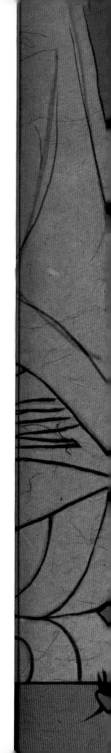

Seized with panic, the three monks hurried to get water with the buckets to put out the fire.

Through their joint effort,
the fire was finally put out.

The three monks came to realize the importance of unity and cooperation. From then on, they had plenty of water to drink everyday.